Alfie Small

UG AND THE DINOSAURS

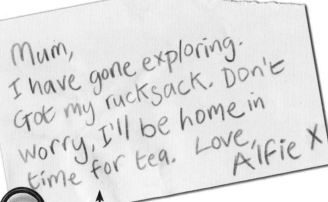

Mum,
I have gone exploring.
Got my rucksack. Don't
worry, I'll be home in
time for tea. Love,
Alfie X

Here's the note I always
leave for Mum before I go
on another adventure

ALFIE SMALL JOURNAL 2: Ug and the Dinosaurs
A DAVID FICKLING BOOK 978 1 849 921206

Published in Great Britain by David Fickling Books,
a division of Random House Children's Books
A Random House Group Company

This edition published 2012

1 3 5 7 9 10 8 6 4 2

DAVID FICKLING BOOKS
31 Beaumont Street, Oxford, OX1 2NP

www.kidsatrandomhouse.co.uk
www.totallyrandombooks.co.uk
www.randomhouse.co.uk

Addresses for companies within The Random House Group Limited can be found at:
www.randomhouse.co.uk/offices.htm

THE RANDOM HOUSE GROUP Limited Reg. No. 954009

A CIP catalogue record for this book is available from the British Library.

Printed in China

Photographs of Alfie's finds by Ian Rycroft. www.ianrycroft.co.uk

MIX
Paper from
responsible sources
FSC® C020056

The Random House Group Limited supports The Forest Stewardship Council (FSC®),the
leading international forest certification organisation. Our books carrying the FSC lable are
printed on FSC® certified paper. FSC is the only forest certification scheme endorsed by
the leading environmental organisations, including Greenpeace. Our paper procurement
policy can be found at www.randomhouse.co.uk/environment

This is the Adventure Journal of

Alfie Small

Hobbies: Exploring and having adventures!

My best friend: Jed

Things I Like: Balloons, Rocky and Ug

Things I Hate: Ogres and Terrible T. Rexes!

1. Up And Away!

This is my → explorer's kit

Jed →

This is me

My name is Alfie Small and I'm a famous explorer. I have lots of dangerous adventures and always take my rucksack of useful things with me. Sometimes, my dog Jed comes along too!

Behind the rickety shed at the bottom of my garden, is the special place I go exploring. The grass is long and the weeds grow thick and I never know what I might find.

Today, I pushed through the weeds . . .
and found a big, stripy balloon with a
wicker basket hanging underneath.

"Come on, Jed!" I cried, jumping into
the basket. I untied a rope, and the
balloon rose high into the sky.

Thick, shifting clouds loomed before us. They formed into the shape of a monstrous ogre's face. Its grinning mouth opened wide and we were swept inside. Jed began to whine.

"Oh, help! Watch out, boy," I cried, as our balloon was buffeted about, and we were thrown around the basket like clothes in a washing machine. Soon I couldn't tell which way was home.

Suddenly, we went spinning out of the cloud. Below us, everything had changed and now we were floating above a strange, rocky landscape.

"Wow! That was a rollercoaster ride, Jed!" I said, but Jed had begun to growl. I turned to see a massive dinosaur-bird streaking through the sky like a rocket.

A prehistoric monster was zooming straight towards us—
HELP!

"A pterodactyl!" I cried in astonishment. Riding on its back was a fierce-looking Stone Age girl. They were heading straight towards us.

"Look out!" I yelled, but it was too late.

BAM! They crashed into our balloon.
"Arrgh!" the girl bellowed angrily.
"Weeark!" screamed the pterodactyl.
It flailed its leathery wings and flew up
and away, ripping a jagged hole in our
balloon. *Whoosh!* Air started rushing
from the tear and we plummeted
towards the ground.

In a panic I opened my rucksack, found my scissors and some string and climbed onto the edge of the basket. I cut a large square of cloth from the flapping balloon and tied lengths of string to each corner. Grasping the strings in one hand, I held Jed in the other and jumped.

"Phew, it works," I cried, as we floated gently down on our homemade parachute. "Looks like we've come to a really dangerous place this time, Jed." And it was just about to get a whole lot worse.

We landed right on top of a giant Tyrannosaurus Rex!

2. One Sore Dinosaur!

"Rarrr!" The terrifying T. Rex shook its mighty head. Jed was thrown off, but as the monster bellowed and bucked I clung on like a rodeo cowboy.

Yeehah!

The earth shook as the dinosaur tried to dislodge me. Jed barked and nipped at the creature's massive, stomping feet. Then the T. Rex ducked its head and roared. The blast sent Jed rolling over the ground.

"Hey!" I yelled, and without thinking, I jumped down to confront the beast. "Pick on someone your own size, pea brain." Uh-oh. Big mistake! The dinosaur opened its huge jaws and I closed my eyes and waited for the crunch!

What a big bully!

"WEEARK!" A loud screech split the air. The T. Rex span around and there, swooping down to land in the clearing was the terrible, swamp-green pterodactyl.

Oh brilliant! I thought. Now they've come back to lend the T. Rex a hand!

Stone Age
← girl

The stocky Stone Age girl leaped from the pterodactyl's back.

"Rocky – attack!" she snarled, pointing at us. The pterodactyl clacked its vicious, bony beak and charged, loping over the ground like a demented giant chicken.

Oh, no!

Rocky

Oh, yikes! Here comes another one

3. Battle Of The Dinosaurs!

But Rocky raced straight past me and dived at the T. Rex. *CRASH!* The two beasts collided in a blur of fangs and talons.

Phew! I thought, my heart hammering with fear and excitement. The pterodactyl isn't after me at all. It's trying to save me!

First it looked as if Rocky was winning. Then the T. Rex clamped its jaws onto the pterodactyl's bony crest.

One of its fangs snapped off, but it wouldn't let go. Rocky needed help!

Slingshot   Swish!

The Stone Age girl unhooked a leather slingshot from her belt and began to fire rocks at the T. Rex, but the beast ignored the hail of stones. I rummaged through my rucksack and found just the thing. A pot of hot pepper!

I sprinted right up to the snarling creatures and threw the spicy powder in the T. Rex's face.

My secret weapon

ALFIE'S EXTRA SNEEZY PEPPER

"Waah!" the beast bellowed, letting go of Rocky. It rubbed its streaming eyes and started to sneeze again and again. Then, with Rocky and Jed snapping at its heels the T. Rex staggered blindly away, bumping into trees and rocks as it went. Phew!

— Me Ug!

The Stone Age girl rushed over to her pet pterodactyl and patted its long bill. Then, turning to me, she gave a wide grin. "Ug!" she said, patting her chest. "Me Ug! You mighty good warrior."

↑ I kept the broken T. Rex's tooth to show Mum

4. Ug!

"Me Alfie Small." I said. Jed barked. "And this is Jed," I added. "Thanks for saving us, Ug!"

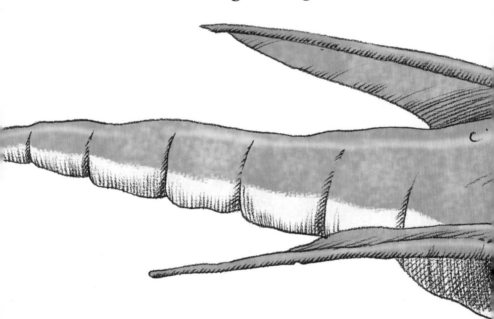

"OK, Alfie Small," said Ug. "Sorry for crash in sky. Was too busy searching ground below. Now, come, we must go before T. Rex return." She climbed onto Rocky's back. I grabbed Jed and clambered up behind her.

"What were you looking for?" I asked.

"My little brother," said Ug. "We out hunting, and Trog was captured by Ogres."

"Ogres? You're joking!" I cried.

"No joke. They deadly enemy of my people," explained Ug, looking around as if she expected one to jump out at us at any moment. "I must rescue Trog, but don't know where him taken."

"What will they do to him?" I gulped.

"Keep him prisoner. Make him work hard all day!"

"The brutes!" I said. "C'mon, what are we waiting for? Let's go and save him. What do these Ogres look like?"

Ug gave a low growl. "Like that," she said and pointed to a nearby hill.

Uh-oh! This doesn't look good

Along the brow of the hill stood a horde of hairy Ogres. They looked very scary. With a loud cry they began swarming down the hill.

"Mustn't get caught," cried Ug, giving Rocky's flank a whack. The pterodactyl leaped into an awkward run. It unfurled its leathery wings, but as it climbed into the sky I toppled off and landed with a heavy bump on the ground!

"Come back!" I cried, as they rose higher and higher. Ug didn't hear me. She had no idea I'd been left behind. Neither did Jed – what a brilliant guard dog he is!

I sat in a daze as the Ogres reached the bottom of the hill. Bellowing like belligerent bulls and swinging great clubs above their heads, they stampeded towards me. The next thing I knew, I was being carried off under a muscly arm.

"Let me go!" I yelled.

5. Prisoner Of The Ogres

I was taken to the Ogres' village and hauled before their chief. He looked like a great, gormless gorilla with spotty blue skin and horrible, hairy nostrils.

"Uh!" he grunted and squeezed the top of my arm. "Weedy!" he muttered. "But will get stronger. Him break rocks with other prisoner."

"Get off, you hairy oaf!" I yelled as another Ogre marched me through the village and into a stone quarry. He left me with a big, burly goon who was guarding just one small boy. The toddler was smashing boulders with a club.

That must be Trog! I thought.

The guard yawned and handed me a club of my own. "Bash!" he ordered pointing at the rocks, and then sat down with his back to the quarry wall.

I dragged the heavy club over to the toddler and started to smash away at the boulders. It was hard work.

"Trog," I whispered as I heaved the club above my head and brought it down with a crash. "I'm Alfie, a friend of Ug's."

"Where Ug?" asked the boy, his eyes wide with excitement. "I want go home."

"She's not here," I said. "But don't worry, I'll help you escape."

"Can't! Too many Ogres," growled Trog, cracking another rock in half.

I glanced over my shoulder. It looked like our guard had dozed off in the warm sunshine. "Let's sneak away while he's asleep," I said.

But the toddler gave me a startled look and shook his head.

"Come on. What's the problem?" I whispered.

"Shush!" hissed Trog. "Work!"

"Don't you want to escape?" I asked.

"No talk, BASH!" thundered a voice, and I span around to see the guard was wide awake and standing right behind me. I was so shocked, I dropped my heavy club – and it landed with a crunch on the Ogre's toes.

"Yeeaagh!" he screamed, leaping up and down and holding his throbbing foot.

"Sorry," I said, but the guard wasn't the forgiving kind.

"Prisoners attack," he cried. "Help!"

"Run!" I yelled, grabbing Trog's hand, but a crowd of Ogres came roaring out of the village and into the quarry.

Oh, yikes! I thought. Now we're in trouble!

"Squish them!" bellowed one Ogre.

"Squash them!" yelled another.

"Put them in pot and cook them," ordered their chief as they surrounded us.

I took my peashooter and a handful of dried peas out of my rucksack.

"I'm Alfie Small, the famous explorer," I crowed. "You're not having me for tea." I fired my peashooter at them again and again, but the Ogres just laughed and swatted the pellets away! With a mighty roar, they surged forwards.

My peashooter

Dried Peas

6. Flight Of The Pterodactyl

Just then I heard a familiar yapping noise.

"Woof! Woof!"

The Ogres stopped in their tracks. "Big, bad wolf!" they gasped and looked nervously around.

A large shadow swept across the ground. I looked up and saw Ug and Jed gliding down on Rocky's back.

"Woof!" yapped Jed.

The pterodactyl's shadow

"Over here!"
I cried, and the
pterodactyl flew
down and seized me in
its talons. I grabbed Trog's
hand, and we were lifted up
into the air. *Yeehah!*
"Arrgh!" roared the furious
Ogres. "Come back!"
"Not likely!" I yelled.

"Well done, Alfie. You save Trog!" said Ug as she pulled us up onto Rocky's back and gave her brother a hug.

"How did you find us?" I asked.

"Was Jed. He sniff you out. Mighty good tracker dog," said Ug, and Jed gave a doggy grin of pleasure!

"We go my house now," said Ug. "I cook you big treat. Boiled mammoth trunk. Yum!"

Oh, yikes! I thought. But just then a delicious smell, from far, far away, drifted through the air. I lifted my nose and sniffed. Mmmm, that's more like it! I thought.

"Er, it sounds delicious, Ug," I said. "But could you take me home instead? Mum's already made my tea."

"Sure," said Ug, and she steered the great lizard-bird up through the swirling clouds. We flew over forests and crossed snow-capped mountains until I saw a patch of tangled weeds below us.

"Down there!" I cried, and Ug sent Rocky wheeling down to land amongst the grasses and thick weeds.

"This for you," said the Stone Age girl, taking the slingshot from her belt and handing it to me. "Better than peashooter, yes?"

"Wow! Much better. Thanks, Ug," I said. Then she grabbed me in a bone-crushing hug, climbed back onto the pterodactyl and took off.

This is the slingshot that Ug gave me

"Bye, Alfie. Bye, Jed," shouted Ug.

"Bye," cried Trog, and we watched them until they were no more than a dot in the sky.

I pushed through the tall and tangled weeds, and came out from behind the shed at the bottom of my garden.

"Alfie, your tea is ready," I heard Mum call.

Mmmm, burgers! I wonder what the Ogres will have for their tea? Not me, that's for sure!

"C'mon, Jed," I cried, and we raced up the garden path.

I am Alfie Small, the famous explorer, and I can't wait for my next amazing adventure to begin.